RUPERT

MEET ALL THESE FRIENDS IN BUZZ BOOKS:

Thomas the Tank Engine
The Animals of Farthing Wood
James Bond Junior
Fireman Sam
Joshua Jones
Rupert
Babar

First published in Great Britain 1993 by Buzz Books,
an imprint of Reed Children's Books
Michelin House, 81 Fulham Road, London, SW3 6RB
and Auckland, Melbourne, Singapore and Toronto

ISBN 1 85591 320 8

Printed in Italy by Olivotto

RUPERT™ and the RHYMING RIDDLE

Story by Norman Redfern
Illustrations by SPJ Design

It was a fine summer's evening. Rupert Bear and Bill Badger had spent their first afternoon on holiday building a sandcastle. Now it was high tide and the waves were lapping at the battlement. Bill picked up a flat, smooth pebble from the shore.

"Watch this," he said.

Bill threw the pebble sideways so that it skimmed across the water, bouncing before it sank below the surface.

"I say, you stop that!"

Rupert turned round to see a smartly dressed man standing behind him.

"That's my yacht over there — the *Lucky Lil* — and I don't want you throwing stones at her!" said the man.

"He wasn't throwing stones at your yacht," Rupert protested.

"Just go away — now!" the man ordered.

Sadly, Rupert and Bill scrambled up to the path above the beach, then stopped to look back at the *Lucky Lil*. Captain Binnacle came down the path from his house and joined them. He had seen the stranger talking to Rupert and Bill.

"I wish I had a yacht like that," said Bill.

"Aye, shipmates, she's a fine vessel," said Captain Binnacle. "Can't say I like her captain much, though."

Rupert told Captain Binnacle how nasty the stranger had been to Bill.

"Never mind," he said. "Rosie, my niece, will be here tomorrow. Why don't I ask her to meet you by those rocks on the beach?"

Next day, Bill and Rupert went to meet the Captain's niece. They clambered over the rocks onto the headland and looked all around, but Rosie was nowhere to be seen.

"Where can she be?" asked Bill.

"Rupert! Bill!"

They looked round again, but could still see no one.

"Over here!" cried Rosie.

There she was, peeping out of a hole in the side of the headland! Rupert and Bill scrambled up to join her.

"It's a cave!" said Rupert.

"Yes," said Rosie, "and there's something in here. Come and look!"

Inside the cave, they found a battered old sea chest. It was padlocked, and there was a crumpled label tied to the handle. In the dim light of the cave, Rupert could just read the writing.

Rosie and Bill listened as Rupert read out the message that was on the label.

"The secret of this treasure chest
Will be yours if you find the key.
So look down below the crow's nest
On the ship that never goes to sea!"

"It's a treasure chest!" gasped Bill. "We must find that key!"

"First, we must solve the rhyming riddle," said Rupert. "The message says the key is hidden below the crow's nest on a ship that never goes to sea. I know a crow's nest is the lookout platform on a ship."

Rosie pointed to the boats bobbing in the little harbour.

"Perhaps it means a ship that never leaves its moorings," she said. "Like a houseboat. Let's go and look!"

Rosie scrambled eagerly over the rocks and ran down the path towards the harbour. She ran up to the Harbour Master, who was outside his hut polishing his brass bell.

"You know all the boats in Rocky Bay, don't you?" she asked.

"No one drops anchor without my say-so," agreed the Harbour Master.

"And," Rosie carried on quickly, "are there any boats which never go to sea?"

"Why yes," he replied. "Old Smuggler Sam hasn't taken the *Sea Breeze* out in years."

Bill, Rosie and Rupert looked at each other. They couldn't believe their luck.

"Smuggler Sam!" they cried.

"Of course, he's not a real smuggler," said the Harbour Master. "He just likes the name."

But Rupert and his friends didn't hear the Harbour Master. They were already searching for the *Sea Breeze*. A little further down the quay, they spotted a wizened man aboard a battered old boat.

"Excuse me," began Rupert. "Could we have a look at your crow's nest, please?"

"Crow's nest?" Smuggler Sam laughed. "This boat's too small for a crow's nest! There's barely room for a seagull to perch up that mast!"

Bill looked very disappointed.

"No crow's nest means no key," he said sadly. "And no key means — "

"No treasure!" said Rupert and Rosie together.

Rupert looked along the row of boats moored in the little bay. None of them had a crow's nest.

"We'll never find the key now," said Bill.

"Let's go back and ask my uncle to help us," said Rosie. "I'm sure he'll know the answer to the riddle."

Rupert, Bill and Rosie walked up the path towards Captain Binnacle's cabin.

Bill pointed to a hotel on the seafront.

"Look! There's the Ship Inn. That's where we're staying," he told Rosie.

Rupert stopped walking.

"The Ship Inn!" he cried. "Now, that's a ship that never goes to sea!"

"Come on, you two!" said Rosie, running down the path. "We'll find the key there. I'm sure we will!"

The three friends ran to the Ship Inn.

"Where's the crow's nest?" asked Bill when they had arrived.

"Follow me," said Rupert.

He led them round to the hotel garden, and pointed up at the old oak tree. High in its branches was a mass of twigs.

"There's the crow's nest!" he said. "The key must be somewhere below it."

Bill rushed forward and reached into a hollow in the side of the tree trunk.

"Is there anything there?" asked Rosie.

The smile on Bill's face grew wider and wider as he pulled out his hand.

"Yes!" he said. "It's a key!"

On the way back to the cave, Bill didn't stop talking.

"What do you think is in that chest?" he asked. "It could be gold! There might be jewels in there. It's bound to be treasure, isn't it?"

At last they reached the cave.

"Try the key in the lock," said Rupert.

Bill turned the key, and with a click the padlock opened. He lifted the lid of the dusty old chest and looked inside. There was something there!

"The riddle says that if you find the key, you can have the treasure," Rupert said. "You found the key, Bill."

"I think we should share the treasure," said Bill firmly.

Bill reached into the chest and carefully lifted out a hand-carved model yacht.

"Let's take it outside," he said.

There, in the warm summer sunshine, Rupert, Bill and Rosie admired the beautiful model boat. Everything about it was perfect — the sails, the rigging, even the name painted on the side.

"She's called the *Lucky Bill*!" said Rosie. "She must be yours, Bill!"

Bill ran down to the water's edge and launched his yacht into the gently bobbing sea.

Rupert and Rosie followed him.

"Rosie," said Rupert, "I'm very glad you discovered that cave."

“Well, my uncle told me where to find it,” replied Rosie.

Captain Binnacle was sitting outside his cabin, carving a piece of wood. He watched Rupert, Bill and Rosie playing with the yacht, and smiled to himself.

RUPERT